Amelia Bedelia

On the Job

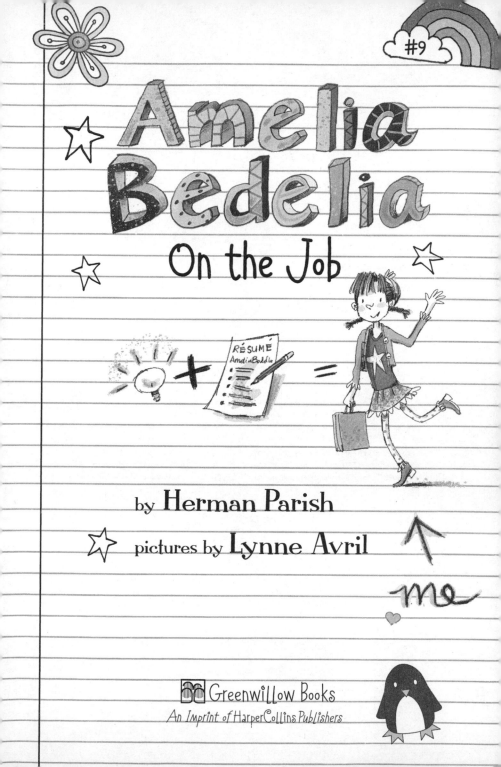

#9

Amelia Bedelia
On the Job

by Herman Parish

pictures by Lynne Avril

↑
me

Greenwillow Books
An Imprint of HarperCollins Publishers

Library of Congress Cataloging-in-Publication Data is available.

ISBN 978-0-06-233413-8 (hardback)—ISBN 978-0-06-233412-1 (pbk. ed.)
"Greenwillow Books."

16 17 18 19 20 CG/RRDH 10 9 8 7 6 5 4 3 2 1 First Edition

 Greenwillow Books

For Philip,

an honest working man—H. P.

To Bernadette,

who is always on the job!—L. A.

Contents

Chapter 1: What Do You Want to Do? 1

Chapter 2: The Hawk Has Landed 9

Chapter 3: "Your Father Was a Jerk!" 20

Chapter 4: Getting Put Through the Mill 31

Chapter 5: What Do Your Parents Do? 38

Chapter 6: These Parks Mean Business 44

Chapter 7: A Tale of Two Nurseries 53

Chapter 8: Lobbying for a Job 60

Chapter 9: Add That to Your Résumé 71

Chapter 10: Draw Your Own Paycheck! 86

Chapter 11: Salad Daze 96

Chapter 12: Tossing Out Ideas to Kick Around 108

Chapter 13: What's the Big Idea? 118

Chapter 14: Do What You Want to Do! 129

Two Ways to Say it 138

Chapter 1

What Do You Want to Do?

Amelia Bedelia was upset. She was *very* upset. What made it even worse was that it was recess. Recess was usually her favorite thing about school! She loved playing on the playground and running around and hanging out with her friends.

"Gotcha!" yelled Clay as he tagged Amelia Bedelia on her back.

Amelia Bedelia jumped straight up in the air. She had been worrying so much, she had forgotten they were in the middle of a game of tag.

"You're it," said Clay, running away.

Instead of chasing everyone, Amelia

Bedelia just stood there and burst into tears.

Daisy raced up and put her arm around Amelia Bedelia's shoulder. "What's wrong?" she asked. "Did Clay hurt you?"

"I barely touched her," said Clay.

"I'm okay," said Amelia Bedelia.

"You don't sound okay," said Daisy. "What's wrong?"

Amelia Bedelia took a deep breath. "You know how Mrs. Shauk told us that we're going to start studying jobs and careers and what we want to do when we grow up?" she asked.

"Yeah," said Cliff. "Sounds like fun, for a change."

"Not to me," said Amelia Bedelia. "I have no idea what I want to be when I grow up."

"That's okay," said Holly. "Neither do I."

Everyone nodded, agreeing with Holly.

"Yeah," said Heather. "You don't have to decide *today* what you're going to be. You

4

have your whole life to figure that out."

"I guess so," said Amelia Bedelia, frowning. "Do you guys know what your parents do? I have no idea what my dad does."

The other kids were quiet. "Does he go to work?" asked Clay.

"Yup. Every day," said Amelia Bedelia. "Last week he came home and said he was pitching to a client."

"Sounds like he plays baseball," said Dawn.

"I thought so, too," said Amelia Bedelia. "Then he said it was a slam dunk. That's basketball, right?"

"Right," said Cliff.

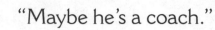

"Maybe he's a coach."

"Maybe," said Amelia Bedelia. "He's always telling the players on TV what they should be doing."

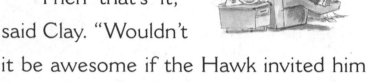

"Then that's it," said Clay. "Wouldn't it be awesome if the Hawk invited him to our class? He could coach us!"

Everyone laughed. It had been a long time since anyone had called Mrs. Shauk by her nickname, the Hawk. She'd earned it because of her ability to spot any kind of mischief or trouble brewing.

"Hey, Cliff," said Amelia Bedelia. "What does your dad do?"

"He's a custodian, or something," said Cliff.

"Your dad doesn't dress like a janitor," said Heather. "He's always wearing a suit when he picks you up."

BRRRRRRR-INNNNNNG!

BRRRRRR-INNNNNNNG! The bell rang to signal that recess was over.

Amelia Bedelia looked at Clay. "Clay, there's one last thing I forgot to tell you," she said softly.

Clay leaned toward Amelia Bedelia so he could hear what she was saying. "What?" he asked.

Amelia Bedelia tapped

him on the shoulder and hollered at the top of her lungs. "YOU'RE IT!"

Amelia Bedelia took off for the school door. Clay chased her, but she raced inside before he could tag her back. The others were running after them, but it is hard to run and laugh at the same time.

8

Chapter 2

The Hawk Has Landed

Mrs. Shauk clapped her hands twice and faced the board. "Amelia Bedelia and Clay, stop sticking your tongues out at each other," she said, with her back to them.

Holly and Heather giggled. Dawn laughed. Cliff made a V sign with his fingers, pointing them at his own eyes and then at Clay, to signal "I'm watching you!" Clay flapped his arms like a bird and called out, *"Awwwk!"* Now nearly everyone was giggling or trying not to, which was harder.

Awwwwk

Mrs. Shauk was still facing the board, and she kept right on writing. "And Clay," she said, "if you'd like to be a bird, you can fly straight to the principal's ofice and perch there for the rest of the day."

Awwwwk

Clay stopped flapping his arms and whirled to face the front of the room with his hands folded neatly on his desk. "Yes, Mrs. Shauk," he said, just as she turned around.

Mrs. Shauk pointed at the board and read aloud what she had just written. "What will you be when you grow up?

"Of course," she continued, "I hope that someday each of you will actually

What will you be when you grow up?

GROW UP

GROW UP

GROW UP

grow up." She glared at Clay, who was studying his hands. Now the whole class was utterly quiet, paying close attention to her every word.

"We are going to study careers and occupations," she said. "Some jobs that you will do haven't even been imagined yet."

"So how can we study them?" asked Chip.

"You can't," said Mrs. Shauk. "Life is changing so fast that new technologies come along all the time. You'll need to be flexible even after you've got a job."

"That's exactly what my dad says," said Wade. "He goes to school two nights

a week, and he works all day at a plant."

Amelia Bedelia could not believe her ears. How could one person work all day at a plant? How much attention did one plant need? Her mom grew lots of plants, and she only worked in her garden every now and then.

"How interesting," said Mrs. Shauk. "Maybe we can set up a field trip to see your dad at work."

That sounded super boring to Amelia Bedelia. All of a sudden, she felt sorry for Wade's dad, standing alone in a big field, tending his one little plant.

"Yes, let's go visit him," said Amelia Bedelia. "He must get very lonely."

"I don't think so," said Wade. "More than forty people work with him."

"Really?" said Amelia Bedelia. "Is there that much to do?"

"Yup," said Wade. "He comes home tired every day."

Amelia Bedelia shook her head. She had a lot to learn about occupations. She tried to picture forty people crowding around one tiny plant. No weed would dare appear with forty people ready to

pounce on it and pull it out. How could any plant even grow? That many people would block out the sun.

"Forty people for one tiny plant?" asked Amelia Bedelia.

"My dad's plant is huge," said Wade.

"It must be," said Amelia Bedelia. "Does it grow up to the sky like in 'Jack and the Beanstalk'?"

For a second, the class was completely silent. Then everyone exploded with laughter.

"Hey, Wade, tell your dad I want to work with him!" yelled Clay. "I'll be like Jack and climb up the beanstalk and steal

the goose that lays golden eggs."

"Me too," yelled Cliff. "Then I won't have to work at all!"

The class laughed even louder. Mrs. Shauk wasn't laughing, but Amelia Bedelia could tell that she was trying really hard not to.

"Okay, everyone!" said Mrs. Shauk, clapping three times to quiet them down. "Amelia Bedelia has given us a good example of how confusing the world of work can be. Every business has its own language, and every profession has its own terms. Don't be afraid to ask questions along the way."

She turned to Clay. "Now, Clay, since you want to work in a plant, please give us a brief report tomorrow. Be sure to tell us what the difference is between a plant and a factory. I would hate for you to show up at the wrong place and miss out on a golden egg."

"Yes, Mrs. Shauk," said Clay.

"And, Cliff," said Mrs. Shauk. "Since your friend Clay will be reporting on plants and factories, I would like you to tell us about mills."

"Mills?" said Cliff, opening his assignment book.

"Yes, mills. Why are some factories called mills?" said Mrs. Shauk. "Steel mills, for example."

"Oh, I thought you meant water mills and windmills," said Cliff.

"You can tell us about those too," said Mrs. Shauk.

Cliff decided to stop talking before his assignment grew any bigger.

Mrs. Shauk had the last word, without saying a word. She made a V sign with her fingers and pointed at Cliff and then at Clay. The whole class got that message.

Amelia Bedelia was happy that Mrs. Shauk had not called on her. She was even happier that she did not get an extra homework assignment. She had heard of water mills and windmills. But the only other mills she knew about were those things in restaurants that waiters used to grind fresh pepper onto salad and pasta. Amelia Bedelia always said, "No, thank you," but her parents always let them do it.

Chapter 3

"Your Father Was a Jerk!"

Dinnertime at Amelia Bedelia's house was like recess, but with food. She couldn't play with her food, of course, because she had to eat it. But that was no problem, because her mom was a great cook.

That night Amelia Bedelia and her parents were talking about where they wanted to go on their next vacation.

They were laughing about everything that had happened on their last vacation, when Amelia Bedelia thought they were going to Rome, Italy, and instead they roamed around in their car.

After the main course (yummy lasagna) Amelia Bedelia's mother served the salad (just like they do in Italy) and her father asked her to pass the pepper.

Then everything clicked: pepper . . . mill . . . factory . . . plant . . . work.

"We are learning about occupations at school," she said, passing the pepper mill to her dad.

"I'm happy to hear that," said her father. "I'm afraid that I'm going to have to do some work tonight after dinner."

"Did you bring work home with you?" asked Amelia Bedelia's mother. She sounded pretty disappointed.

"Sorry, honey," he said, shrugging.

Amelia Bedelia was not disappointed. This was a clue! If her dad brought work home with him, that meant his job fit into the little satchel he carried every day.

Amelia Bedelia and her father usually

did the dishes and cleaned up after dinner, but tonight Amelia Bedelia's mother helped out so that her father could do what he needed to do. As soon as the dining room table was cleared, he spread out some notes and papers, opened his laptop, and went to work.

While she rinsed the dishes and loaded the dishwasher, Amelia Bedelia peeked in at her dad, trying to get a glimpse of what

he was doing. She thought of a question she had always wanted to ask her mom.

"Where did you meet Dad?" asked Amelia Bedelia.

"I met your father at work," said her mom. "Back then, he was a jerk."

"What?" called Amelia Bedelia's father from the dining room.

"Sorry, sweetie!" Amelia Bedelia's mother called back. "We didn't mean to disturb you. What I meant was that you were a *real* jerk."

"Honey!" Amelia Bedelia's father bounded into the kitchen. "What are you talking about?"

Before Amelia Bedelia's mother could even open her mouth, her father said, "Once upon a time, way back when your mother and I were in high school, we both worked in the same drugstore."

"Did you sell medicine and beach toys and candy?" asked Amelia Bedelia.

"Well, I ran the cash register," said Amelia Bedelia's mother.

"And I was in charge of the soda fountain," said Amelia Bedelia's father. "There used to be soda fountains everywhere, and the old-fashioned drugstore

in our town still had one. I made sodas using various flavors of ice cream. To add the soda water, I had to jerk a handle back and forth, like this—" He swung his hand to demonstrate. "Anyone who made sodas like that was called a 'soda jerk.'"

"Jerk, for short," said her mother.

"Jerk Forshort?" said Amelia Bedelia, struggling to keep a straight face. Then she burst out laughing. "Dad, you've told some giant fibs before, but that was a whopper— you are making that up!" As  her chuckles began to subside, she noticed that her father was not laughing. In fact, he looked a little hurt.

"It's true, sweetie," said her mother, smiling. "Your dad was well known as a jerk. He once won a cream-soda contest."

"That's *Mister* Jerk to you," said Amelia Bedelia's father, kissing her mother on the cheek. "I met your mom in the store. I won her heart with a banana split made with so much rocky road ice cream that it cost me a week's wages."

"That was the best investment you

ever made," said Amelia Bedelia's mother.

Her parents hugged and kissed again. Amelia Bedelia got up and put her arms around them for a family hug. This totally explained her dad's weakness for rocky road ice cream, she thought.

"Ah, well," said Amelia Bedelia's father. "That was a fun trip down memory lane. Now I have to get back to work on some slides."

That gave Amelia Bedelia another

important clue about what her father did for a living. He had already put together the slide for her swing set years ago, so he wasn't working on that kind of slide.

Then she remembered how excited her father got when ballplayers on TV would slide into second base or home plate. So . . . Dawn had been right about

baseball. That must be the kind of slide he was working on, a baseball slide.

But how could he be working on those kinds of slides on his computer? If he slid into his laptop, he might break it. Maybe her dad was writing instructions on how to slide and score without being tagged out. So, Cliff had been right too. Her father must be a coach—a baseball coach. Now that was a job she could be proud of.

She certainly wasn't going to tell her class that her father was an award-winning jerk.

Chapter 4

Getting Put Through the Mill

The next morning Clay gave his report about plants and factories. "The word 'plant' is used to describe any place where things are manufactured (that means 'made'). The word 'factory' is actually short for manufacturing plant. Facturing, factory. Get it? So the words 'plant'

and 'factory' actually mean the same thing.
A lot of times, in a plant or factory, things
are made on an assembly line."

"Good job, Clay," said Mrs. Shauk.
"Very nice."

Clay broke into a big smile and sat back
down in his seat.

Amelia Bedelia remembered dancing in a conga line at an assembly, but that line only made kids smile.

Mrs. Shauk turned to Cliff and said, "Cliff, can you tell us why some factories are called—"

"Or plants," interrupted Clay.

"Factories or plants," repeated Mrs. Shauk, "are called mills? That is, unless you've amassed enough money since yesterday to retire?"

Cliff stood up and cleared his throat. "Water running in rivers and streams provided the power for many of the first factories or plants," he said. "For example, water power was used to grind—or mill—grain into flour for making bread. The place where the grain was ground became known as a flour mill. When water was used to power other types of machinery, to make different things, the name 'mill' stuck. That's why today we have steel mills and paper mills, even though they are not

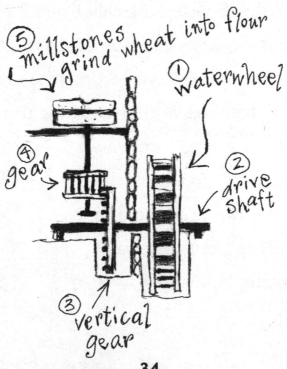

⑤ millstones grind wheat into flour

① waterwheel

④ gear

② drive shaft

③ vertical gear

powered by water anymore."

"Excellent, Clifford!" said Mrs. Shauk, clapping her hands. A couple of other kids applauded along with her, including Amelia Bedelia. Cliff bowed.

"Now, before you sit down," said Mrs. Shauk, "please share with the class what your mother and father do for work. Then we'll go around the room and hear what everyone's parents do."

Cliff cleared his throat again and said, "I think my dad is a janitor."

"You think?" asked Mrs. Shauk, looking confused. "Are you sure that your father is a custodian?"

"Yup. Pretty sure," said Cliff. "That's how he talks about his job."

"Ha! I see," said Mrs. Shauk as Cliff sat down.

Amelia Bedelia slipped down in her seat, trying to shrink out of sight so that the Hawk would fly right over her and dive on a different victim. But Mrs. Shauk could be sly. She was looking right at Dawn when she called out, "Amelia Bedelia!"

"Yeeeeha!" shouted Amelia Bedelia, jumping up as if her bottom had been pricked by a thumbtack. "I mean, yes, Mrs. Hawk."

Mrs. Shauk narrowed her eyes. "Please share with the class a little bit about your parents' occupations," she said.

Amelia Bedelia started swaying back and forth. She looked like she was trying to get her timing right before hopping in to join someone who was already jumping rope. The voice in her brain kept repeating, *What do I say? What do I say? What do I say?*

"My father is a coach," said Amelia Bedelia finally.

Chapter 5

What Do Your Parents Do?

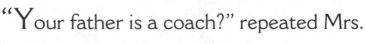

"Your father is a coach?" repeated Mrs. Shauk. "What does he coach?"

"Baseball?" said Amelia Bedelia.

"Baseball?" said Mrs. Shauk. "Ha!"

"And basketball," added Amelia Bedelia.

"Ha! *Ha-ha-ha-ha-ha!*" said Mrs. Shauk.

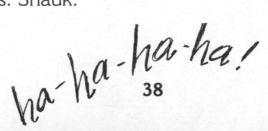

Why was the Hawk laughing? Now some of the other kids were laughing too. Amelia Bedelia wondered what would have happened if she'd said her dad was a jerk. Everyone would probably be rolling around on the floor by now. She sat back down in her seat.

"I'm sorry, Amelia Bedelia," said Mrs. Shauk, wiping the tears out of her eyes.

1,021   1,022   1,023
1,024
1,025

"I apologize for laughing. I'm not laughing at you or your father. I don't have to tell you what a great guy he is. I was laughing at myself . . . because when I was your age, I thought that my father counted beans for a living."

"Magic beans?" asked Clay.

"No, just ordinary beans," said Mrs. Shauk. "I thought he counted beans, day in and day out."

"What did he really do?" asked Holly.

"He was an accountant," said Mrs. Shauk. "He helped people keep track of the money in their businesses. He always called himself a bean counter. My mother said he was an accountant, but I thought

slang

40

she meant he was a-counting beans. 'Bean counter' is a slang term."

"What's a slang term?" asked Rose.

It seemed that Mrs. Shauk hadn't heard Rose's question. "Take out your assignment books," she said. "Now I want you to write down what you think your mother and father do for a living."

Amelia Bedelia was pretty confused. She almost wrote down "breathe," because isn't that what everyone does to keep living? But she decided to write "coach" for her father and "everything" for her mother. When she looked up, she couldn't help but notice that most kids hadn't written down anything at all.

"All done?" asked Mrs. Shauk. "Good. Now, tonight at dinner, or whenever your mother and father get home, just ask them what they do for a living. What's their job? Their occupation? What do they do every day? How long have they been doing it? What do they like best and least about it? Did they have to go to school to learn what they do? What sort of training did they get?"

"You want us to interview our parents like we're reporters on TV?" asked Heather.

"Exactly," said Mrs. Shauk. "I think you and your classmates may be surprised by what you discover."

Rose was closing her assignment book when Mrs. Shauk added, "Oh, Rose, first thing tomorrow, please give us a report on the word 'slang,' with examples."

Chapter 6

These Parks Mean Business

When Amelia Bedelia's mother picked her up after school, she had a surprise for Amelia Bedelia. "Dad is getting off early from work today," she said. "So we're going to swing by and pick him up too."

Amelia Bedelia hadn't visited her dad's office since she was super little, and she didn't really remember much about it. As they got closer, they drove by big signs that Amelia Bedelia read out loud: "Business Park . . . Office Park . . ."

Amelia Bedelia saw lots of trees, grass, bushes, and flowers. She did not see any slides or swings or play structures, just buildings that looked like big boxes. Amelia Bedelia figured that the parks must be indoor parks, and all the fun stuff must be inside those buildings.

She kept hoping she'd see a sign that said BALLPARK. Instead she saw one that said PROFESSIONAL PARK. *Wow,* she

thought. Her town must be pretty great if it had a *professional* park. That sounded almost as important as a national park. In science class, they had learned about the national parks, including Yosemite—with its giant waterfalls and redwood trees—

and Yellowstone—with bears and Old Faithful.

The professional park sign made her wonder about the other parks in her town. Were those

Giant Redwoods

Old Faithful
YELLOWSTONE PARK

amateur parks? She loved the park near her house, even if it was unprofessional.

"After we get Daddy, can we please play in the professional park?" she asked.

"These parks are not for playing," said Amelia Bedelia's mother. "They're for working." She made a right turn. "Here we are. Corporate Park."

They pulled in front of a group of buildings made of shiny glass. Her dad walked out of the tallest one.

"Hi, guys," said Amelia Bedelia's father, getting into the car. He kissed Amelia Bedelia's mother on the cheek and blew a kiss to Amelia Bedelia in the backseat.

"How was your day, honey?" asked Amelia Bedelia's mother.

"Great!" he said. "Remember those

slides I was working on last night? They were a big hit. I scored a lot of points today."

That sounded like baseball to Amelia Bedelia. Maybe she was right!

"I have an idea," said Amelia Bedelia's mother. "Let's have an early dinner and go for a bike ride." She looked in the rearview mirror at Amelia Bedelia. "Do you have much homework, sweetie?"

Homework!

"We are learning about occupations," said Amelia Bedelia. "We're supposed to interview our parents about what they do."

"I'll go first," said Amelia Bedelia's mother. "I'm a homemaker. That means I do everything." She laughed.

"That is so true," said Amelia Bedelia's father, nodding his head. "And because your mother does such an amazing job, I am able to focus on my job."

"But what do you do?" said Amelia Bedelia.

"Marketing," said her father.

"Daddy, Mom does the marketing," said Amelia Bedelia. "You hardly ever buy groceries."

"Marketing is about selling things," said Amelia Bedelia's father, turning around in his seat to face her. "It could be anything, a car or a can of soup. I help people figure out  what to say about what they have to sell."

"Is that like being a coach?" asked Amelia Bedelia.

"You could say that," said her father.

"I just did," said Amelia Bedelia.

Amelia Bedelia was relieved that her father was some kind of a coach. She kept asking her parents questions, because it was fun to hear them talk about the different kinds of jobs they had had and what they had learned from them and all the different types of people they had worked with.

"Did either of you ever work in a factory?" asked Amelia Bedelia.

"Say again?" said her father.

"Or plant," said Amelia Bedelia.

"No, sweetie," said her mother. "The only plants I'm interested in are the vegetables in my garden. Now that you are getting older, though, I have been thinking about going back to work."

"What would you do?" asked Amelia Bedelia.

"*Hmmm,*" her mother said. "I think I'll surprise you."

Chapter 7

A Tale of Two Nurseries

The next day Rose stood in front of the class to give her report about slang words. "We all use slang words every day. Slang words are words or expressions that we use when we talk to our friends in a casual way. Groups of people also use slang words. For example, slang terms for an accountant are 'bean counter' or 'number cruncher.'"

Mrs. Shauk laughed. "I had forgotten about crunching numbers. My father used to say that too."

Amelia Bedelia wondered how to crunch a number. Would that be fun? Was that how fractions were made?

"Slang can be used to describe whole groups of workers," said Rose. "People with professions, like people in law and business, are called white-collar workers because their shirts are usually white, at least they were in the olden times. People with a trade or skill, like plumbers and electricians, are called blue-collar workers for the same reason, except the color is different."

"Excellent, Rose," said Mrs. Shauk. "Speaking of law, Cliff, did you find out what your father does?"

"Yup," said Cliff. "My dad is a lawyer."

"Not the same as a custodian," said Mrs. Shauk.

"It's not my fault," said Cliff. "Last night he came home and said, 'Messes! All I do is clean up messes!' And when I asked him about his job, he explained that the messes he was talking about were legal problems that people have. By helping them figure things out, he is cleaning up those messes."

Drew, the boy sitting in front of Amelia Bedelia, said, "My mother works in a nursery."

"I love babies," said Amelia Bedelia.

Drew laughed. "So does my mom, but she works in the nursery at a garden center. She takes care of thousands of seedlings. She calls them her babies."

Haley, who sat behind Amelia Bedelia, said, "My mother works in the nursery at the hospital, taking care of newborns."

"Both of your mothers work in nurseries, but those are very different jobs," said Mrs. Shauk. "How are they similar?"

Angel raised her hand. "A baby seedling and a real baby both need to be taken care of and protected," she said.

"Right!" said Mrs. Shauk. "That applies to your ideas too. Many great ideas need to be protected and nurtured before people recognize how good they are and accept them."

Finally, it was Amelia Bedelia's turn. "My mother does

everything. She's a homemaker."

"Mr. Shauk is a homemaker too," said Mrs. Shauk. "And, Amelia Bedelia, is your father really a coach?"

"Sort of," said Amelia Bedelia. "He coaches people on how to sell things, not play things. He calls it marketing, but it's not just in the supermarket."

"Cool," said Clay. "Does he make TV commercials?"

"My mom works in advertising," said Heather. "Does your dad think up coupons and promotions?"

"My father just got

promoted," said Amelia Bedelia.

"Then he must be doing a good job," said Mrs. Shauk. "Okay, everyone, these are all great questions and comments. Let's keep thinking like that, because I have a surprise for you. We're going to visit some real workplaces. First up is the professional park where Amelia Bedelia's father works. So your assignment tonight is to think up some questions for him."

"What color is his collar?" asked Rose.

"Today it was white with little blue stripes," said Amelia Bedelia.

"So he's a white- *and* blue-collar worker," said Clay. "Cool."

Chapter 8

Lobbying for a Job

Things were a little wackier than usual at Amelia Bedelia's house on the morning of the field trip to her father's office. For one thing, her mother was already out working in her garden, even though the sun was barely up. By the time Amelia Bedelia had gotten dressed and gone down to the kitchen for breakfast, the refrigerator was full of fresh, just-picked lettuce.

"Are we having a salad for breakfast?" asked Amelia Bedelia, looking at the wall of green leaves.

"That's for later," said her mother, handing her a bowl of cereal.

Amelia Bedelia's class took a bus to the office where her father worked. The building was so shiny that it reflected the trees and sky like a giant mirror. Everyone gathered at the entrance and made goofy faces at their reflections while Mrs. Shauk gave instructions to the bus driver. A man wearing a blue jumpsuit approached, squirted something onto the glass, and wiped it off, making the glass even shinier.

"Thanks," said Amelia Bedelia. "You must work here."

"Only once a month," said the man. "My partner and I clean all the windows on the outside of this building."

"Wow!" said Amelia Bedelia.

The man climbed onto a scaffold and put on a safety harness. "I do the opposite of what people in business do," he said. "I go straight to the top and then work my way down." His partner pushed a lever. An electric winch hummed and up they went, heading for the top of the building. "You kids should take the elevator instead," he yelled, waving. "See you upstairs!"

Mrs. Shauk herded everyone inside and across the lobby to the security desk. Lots of people were moving back and forth across the shiny marble floor. Some were

63

strolling, some running, but most just walked. When everyone crowded around the desk, a woman in a uniform looked up from a bunch of screens and said, "You must be here for the school visit."

"How did you know?" asked Amelia Bedelia.

"It's my job," she said. "I check people into the building and help visitors find where they want to go." She picked up a phone with one hand and took a thick

envelope from a deliveryman with the other. "Your visitors have arrived," she said into the receiver.

Wade looked at the deliveryman. "Is your job fun?" he asked.

"It varies," said the deliveryman. "Last night it was picking up, this morning it's dropping off. I rush around a lot." He handed the security guard a clipboard. "I need your autograph here, please."

The guard smiled, signed her name, and returned the clipboard. Amelia Bedelia had never seen anyone give an autograph before. She knew that only important or famous people got asked for their autographs. "Are you famous?" she

asked. "May I have your autograph too?"

The guard laughed and signed the first page in the small notebook that Amelia

Bedelia gave her. On the bus, Mrs. Shauk had handed out one to each student, so they could all take notes about the field trip. "They are waiting for you on the sixteenth floor," the guard said, handing Mrs. Shauk a sheet of sticky name tags. "You're all signed in—just wear these badges while you are in the building."

"Meet me at the bank of elevators," said Mrs. Shauk, sticking an ID badge on each of her students.

Amelia Bedelia followed her friends across the lobby. She had heard of a bank for savings. She had a piggy bank in her room at home. Her parents used a bank for writing checks. And she loved sandbanks.

She had no clue what a bank of elevators might look like.

Luckily, there was an ATM

in the wall by one of the elevators, so Amelia Bedelia stood next to it. A cash machine was almost a bank.

"You cannot use this elevator right now. It's going out of service. I have to inspect it," said a man wearing green coveralls and carrying a small tool kit.

"Why do you need to inspect it?" asked Amelia Bedelia.

"That's my job," said the man. "I make

sure that elevators operate safely."

"Do you like inspecting elevators?" asked Amelia Bedelia.

"It has its ups and downs," he said, smiling.

At last Mrs. Shauk managed to get the entire class onto two working elevators.

Cliff and Clay were on one; Amelia Bedelia was on the other.

"Hey, Amelia Bedelia!" the boys shouted. "Let's race!"

Amelia Bedelia pressed the button with the number sixteen on it, and up they went.

Chapter 9

Add That to Your Résumé

Both elevators arrived on the sixteenth floor at the exact same time. The doors opened, and everyone stepped out into another lobby. It was smaller but nicer, with thick carpeting, fancy chairs, and a comfy-looking couch.

"Here you are," said a young woman with a friendly smile. "I have been waiting

for you. My name is Miss Sanderson, but you can call me Sandy for short."

"Hi, Sandy Forshort," said Amelia Bedelia. "I'm Amelia Bedelia. You can call me Amelia Bedelia."

Sandy laughed. "Aha! Your father works here, right?" she said. "You have the same sense of humor. Now, if you please, follow me into the conference room and we'll get started."

The conference room was spacious and bright. There were just enough chairs for everyone to have a seat around a long table.

"Welcome to the Idea Group," said Sandy. "We help businesses advertise and market their products. Our goal is for

people to learn good things about products so that they choose to buy them."

"Is that what you do all day?" asked Joy.

"No," said Sandy. "I work in human relations."

"I am a human related to my dad," said Amelia Bedelia.

Sandy laughed again. "You sure are," she said. "But you don't have to be related to someone to work here. We employ all sorts of smart people, just like you guys."

"Are you offering us jobs?" said Holly.

"Not yet," said Sandy. "You need a few more years of school. Education will automatically open doors for you."

"Like walking into a supermarket?"

asked Amelia Bedelia.

"It's not that easy," said Sandy, smiling. "Education just helps you get your foot in the door."

"What about the rest of me?" asked Amelia Bedelia.

"Let's talk about all of you," said Sandy. "This morning you are going to work on writing a résumé."

"Is that a different language?" asked Wade.

"It's a French word for 'summary,'" said Sandy.

"What's French for 'wintery'?" asked Amelia Bedelia.

résumé
=
summary

"*Hivernal*," said Mrs. Shauk. "Now stop interrupting Sandy so she can share what she has planned for you."

"*Merci!*" said Sandy to Mrs. Shauk.

"I was a French major," explained Mrs. Shauk. "Now, I want everyone to sit up straight and pay attention. I'll be back shortly."

Amelia Bedelia was impressed. No wonder Mrs. Shauk was so tough. She had been a major in the French army!

Sandy picked up a stack of paper and began handing out one sheet to each student. "Right now I am going to pass out—"

She stopped and looked at Cliff and Clay, who were spinning around and around in their chairs.

Amelia Bedelia sprang into action.

"Help!" she hollered. "Sandy is going to pass out!" She jumped up and gently pushed Sandy down into her chair. Sandy was shocked speechless.

"Penny! Quick!" yelled Amelia Bedelia. "What do we do next?"

Everyone knew that Penny was going to be a doctor when she grew up.

"Elevate her feet!" yelled Penny.

"Impossible!" said Amelia Bedelia.

"The elevator is way back in the lobby."

"Let's get her feet up!" said Penny.

"I'm fine!" said Sandy, as the girls each grabbed one of her legs.

"Hold on!" said Sandy.

"Right, hold on!" said Amelia Bedelia.

"One!" said Penny.

"Two!" said Amelia Bedelia.

"Three!" yelled Penny and Amelia Bedelia together as they lifted Sandy's feet into the air. *Stop!*

"Stop!" yelled Sandy. "I'm okay!"

Just then, Mrs. Shauk came back into the conference room. "What in the world?" she blurted out, rushing to Sandy's side.

It took several minutes for everyone to

Stop!

get untangled and explain to Mrs. Shauk what had happened.

"That was certainly an adventure," said Sandy, smiling. Her hair was ruffled, but she didn't seem mad at all. "Now, I want you to write your profile on this sheet of paper."

Mrs. Shauk leaned over and whispered in Amelia Bedelia's ear. "Listen to Sandy and do exactly what she says. No ifs, ands, or buts, please."

Amelia Bedelia grabbed her marker and sat up straight.

"Write down your name and all the things you would like someone to know about you if they were going to hire you for a job," Sandy continued. "For example,

Name:_____

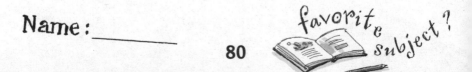

what is your favorite subject in school? What sports do you play? Do you play an instrument or like to draw or paint? Have you done work for your community? Ever had a job? What you put down should be as individual as you are, like a fingerprint. I should be able to tell who you are right away by looking at your profile."

Amelia Bedelia put her head down on the table. She turned so that the left side of her face rested on her sheet of paper. Then she took the marker and carefully traced her profile. She drew from the top of her head down to the tip of her nose, made a sharp turn, then bumpity-bumped past her lips, took an upsy-daisy

around her chin, and then finished up just a little way down her neck. She sat up and looked around. Everyone else was busy writing.

"Cat naps are great, aren't  they, Amelia Bedelia?" said Sandy, shaking her head. "Are you ready to begin your profile?"

"I'm done," said Amelia Bedelia. She glanced quickly around the conference room, searching for a cat, but she didn't see one.

Sandy studied Amelia Bedelia's profile.

"My nose needs a little work, but there I am, see?" said Amelia Bedelia.

"That's totally you, Amelia Bedelia," said Sandy. "And you certainly are a piece

83

of work." She smiled. "Now let's get you started on the rest of your profile."

When everyone had finally finished, Sandy read a few of the profiles out loud and asked the class to guess which kids the profiles were describing. She read Amelia Bedelia's last. The more she read, the higher her eyebrows arched. "Wait, wait, wait," she said, raising her hand in the air. "Let me see if I've got this straight. You walked dogs and won a prize at a dog show?"

"Oh, the dog won, not me," said Amelia Bedelia.

"Noted," said Sandy. "You got a wreath at the school Olympics, helped

build a community park, erected a zoo in your backyard, and won a fishing contest, all while running a small business selling lemon tarts?"

Amelia Bedelia nodded, along with the rest of the class, including Mrs. Shauk.

"Well done," said Sandy. "Your résumé is full of accomplishments. Keep up the good work. One day you may be the president."

"Of the company?" asked Amelia Bedelia.

"Of the country!" said Sandy.

"*Sacre bleu!*"* said Mrs. Shauk.

---

* A French expression of surprise, like "Holy smoke!"

Chapter 10

Draw Your Own Paycheck!

When the students returned to the conference room after a bathroom and water break, they found a young man with really short red hair standing next to Sandy. The two were chatting and laughing.

"Is everybody back?" asked Sandy. "Great, now that you've all got a head start on your résumés, you may be wondering

how much money you'll make when you start working and how you'll manage your expenses. To answer that question, I am happy to introduce you to a close friend of mine from the finance department. This is Andy Miles, and he's going to talk with you about his favorite subject—accounting."

The class clapped politely. Andy
waved hello and heaved a cloth sack
onto the table. It landed with a thud.
The words FIRST NATIONAL BANK were
written on it. He turned the bag over
and dumped a heap of penny
rolls onto the table. He
rolled a roll of pennies to
each student.

"Hey, thanks!" said Teddy.

"I'm rolling your pay to you because I
work in payroll," said Andy. "Get it?"

"Got it," said Amelia Bedelia, catching
her roll of pennies. "Are we going to count
beans and crunch numbers now?"

Andy threw his head back and
laughed.

"I'm to blame for that comment," said Mrs. Shauk. "My father was an accountant, so I shared those slang terms."

"There are lots of slang terms in accounting," said Andy. "My favorite is calling money cabbage or kale or lettuce . . . because they are all leafy and green."

Amelia Bedelia imagined pouring salad dressing over a bowl of dollar bills. *Yuck!*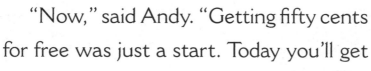

"Now," said Andy. "Getting fifty cents for free was just a start. Today you'll get to actually draw a paycheck. How does that sound!"

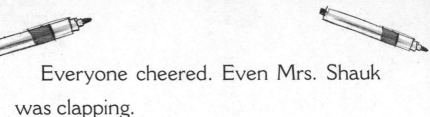

Everyone cheered. Even Mrs. Shauk was clapping.

"Listen up," said Andy, reaching into the bank bag and pulling out a handful of markers in all different colors. "When you draw a paycheck, that's slang for *withdraw*. Most companies pay their employees every two weeks with a check that lets them withdraw money from the company's bank account. That's how people get paid. And the amount you get paid helps determine how much you can spend or save. Today is the only chance you'll ever get to draw your own paycheck."

"Do you have any red markers?" asked Teddy.

XAKAHHAGGG!!

"AAAAHHHHGGGG!" bellowed Andy. He shut his eyes and put his hands in front of his face like a vampire who has seen the sun. Peeking through his fingers, he said, "Accountants are afraid of red ink. We use red ink only to show when money is being lost. We hate being 'in the red.' We always want to be 'in the black,' because that means we have made a profit."

Everyone grabbed markers and paper and got to work.

Teddy drew a big dollar sign and the number one with a comma after it, then three zeros, another comma, three more zeros, comma, another three zeros, comma,

three zeroes . . .

"Nineteen, twenty, twenty-one . . . ," said Teddy, counting the zeros.

"What are you doing?" asked Amelia Bedelia.

"Trying to figure out how big my paycheck is," said Teddy.

"Just count the commas," Rose said.

"A thousand has one, a million has two,

a billion has three, a trillion has—"

"How do you spell a skrillion dollars?" asked Clay.

"I'm adding as many commas and zeros as I can fit," said Heather.

Amelia Bedelia drew her paycheck to look like exactly like money. "That way," she said, "if I have trouble cashing it, I can always just spend it."

"Of course," said Andy. "Now that

93

you've drawn your own paycheck, the only place you can cash it is the First National Bank of Y-O-U."

"Is that like an I-Owe-You?" asked Dawn.

"Sounds more like a You-Owe-You," said Chip.

"Exactly—" said Andy.

There was a knock on the door of the conference room. When Sandy opened it, Andy looked out and declared, "Gosh, I've never seen so much lettuce in my life! They have to wheel it in!"

"How much is it?" asked Dawn. "Hundreds? Thousands?"

"At least ten," said Amelia Bedelia's father. "Ten heads of lettuce."

He was followed by Amelia Bedelia's mother, wheeling a cart laden with a giant bowl of salad. "Lunchtime!" she said.

"Adios," said Andy, giving the students a giant wave that included everybody. "Good luck, and don't spend all that lettuce in one place!"

Chapter 11

Salad Daze

Amelia Bedelia's mother filled individual bowls to the brim with lettuce. There were interesting types, with a variety of colors and textures.

"I'll pass out . . ." Sandy started to say. "I mean, *hand* out the salads."

Amelia Bedelia's father stood at the front of the room.

"Okay, kids! I am Amelia Bedelia's

father, as all of you know. Thank you for visiting!" He began pacing back and forth. "We ordered pizza, but they are running late. So, we are going to start with salad first, like normal families do. Not like at my house, where we eat our salad last." He winked at Amelia Bedelia.

"You eat salad for dessert?" said Clay, snorting.

"Yucko, Bedelia!" snuffled Cliff.

"Enough!" said Mrs. Shauk.

Amelia Bedelia's cheeks burned. "No,"

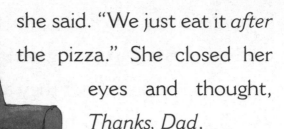

she said. "We just eat it *after* the pizza." She closed her eyes and thought, *Thanks, Dad.*

"I'm really sorry," said Amelia Bedelia's father. "Here you are in your salad days, and I was assuming that you all like to eat salad. How many absolutely hate salad?"

Three boys and one girl raised their hands.

Amelia Bedelia hoped this salad day would not last too much longer.

"Thanks for being honest," he said. "Would you be willing to try a bit of salad today?"

Everyone nodded.

"Thank you," he said. "Now, I don't want you to start eating until you get these two little containers of salad dressing." He held the containers up, then began handing them out. One was orange and the other was purple.

When each student had a salad and the two dressings, Amelia Bedelia's father said, "Pour one dressing on half your salad and the other dressing on the other half. Don't mix them. Then take a bite from each side."

When they had all done that, Amelia

Bedelia's father asked them to vote for their favorite flavor. The orange containers won by two votes.

"Now I know that absolutely no one here plays with their food. But today I want you to play 'what if' with your food," said Amelia Bedelia's father.

"What if what?" asked Dawn.

"What if these salad dressings were athletes," said Amelia Bedelia's father. "What sport would they play? Think about that as you take another bite of each one." The kids looked at one another and did that.

"The orange one would play football, and the purple one would play soccer," said Pat.

"The orange one is spicier and different," said Daisy. "It would play lacrosse or something unusual."

Amelia Bedelia's father wrote that down and then asked, "What if these dressings listened to music? What kind would they like? What would their favorite song be? Who is their favorite performer?"

Everyone began talking immediately.

"Hang on, hang on! Take another taste, then talk," said Amelia Bedelia's father.

"And don't talk with your mouths full, please," said Mrs. Shauk.

101

The kids chewed, swallowed, then dove into a discussion about music mixed with salad dressing. Everyone had ideas and comments and strong opinions, and Amelia Bedelia's father was taking notes as fast as he could.

"If these dressings were superheroes," he said when the room was quiet again, "what amazing power would they have?"

"They'd make me want to eat salad," said Dawn. She was the only girl who hadn't liked salad. The boys who didn't like salad nodded in agreement.

"If you guys had either of these

dressings at home, would you eat more salads?" asked Amelia Bedelia's father.

The non-salad eaters all nodded yes.

"I always give credit where credit is due," said Amelia Bedelia's father. "These dressings were created by Amelia Bedelia's mother. Everything was organic, including the lettuce she grew in her garden."

"Delicious!" said Mrs. Shauk, applauding. Soon everyone else was clapping. Amelia Bedelia was embarrassed, but in a good way. She noticed that her mother was blushing too.

"Okay!" said Amelia Bedelia's father. "I think it's time for lunch."

"Wait a minute. Aren't you going to tell us what you do?" asked Teddy.

"I just showed you," said Amelia Bedelia's father. "When was the last time you talked about salad dressing or even thought about it?"

"Never," said Teddy.

"That's right," said Amelia Bedelia's father. "Most people never do. But if you have great-tasting salad dressings like these, and you want people—especially kids—to give them a try, you've got to learn what kids like and want and how to talk to them. That's what marketing is all about. It's mostly common sense."

There was a knock on the conference-room door. Amelia Bedelia's father opened it and held it open for a delivery guy carrying a big stack of pizza boxes. Amelia Bedelia's father closed his eyes and inhaled deeply as the pizzas passed by him. "Naturally," he said, "one of the best

ways to get people to try your product is simply to give out samples. I can illustrate this again with the pizzas. Let's dig in!"

Mrs. Shauk, Sandy, and Amelia Bedelia's father served slices to everyone in the class, then helped themselves.

Amelia Bedelia's father soon had them all talking about pizza as easily as they had talked  about salad dressings. They talked about toppings and crust and cheese. Kids began recalling commercials that they liked and why they liked them. Then Amelia Bedelia's dad began telling stories about his work. Amelia Bedelia was amazed at all the funny, weird, crazy, and ridiculous things that had happened to him on the

job. He made her classmates laugh, and he made working sound like fun, instead of work. No one would ever guess that he had started off as a jerk.

"Hey, Amelia Bedelia!" said Clay, slurping a huge piece of cheese off his slice of pizza. "Your dad is so cool!"

Chapter 12

Tossing Out Ideas to Kick Around

Once lunch had been cleared away, Sandy handed out paper and scattered markers in the middle of the table.

"Okay," said Sandy. "We've been talking about work and our jobs. Now we'd like to hear from you. How can we improve things? What are you hoping to find in a job? What sort of business would you start? Write down what you're thinking or feeling. Toss out a bunch of ideas so we can kick them around."

"Will they get hurt?" asked Amelia Bedelia. "Will you throw them out?"

"Yeah," said Angel. "Mrs. Shauk says that good ideas are fragile and need to be protected."

"Like a young plant," said Holly.

"Or a newborn," said Heather.

"You wouldn't kick those around, would you?" said Amelia Bedelia.

"Of course not," said Sandy. "Pardon my jargon. Tossing out ideas and kicking them around is how we describe sharing our thoughts and ideas and working together to improve them."

"Angel, I'll be looking for a report on the difference between jargon and slang next week," said Mrs. Shauk.

"Don't hold back," said Sandy. "No idea is too wild or crazy. It may spark another idea from someone else. You just never know! Your ideas should be outside the box—whoops!" She covered her mouth with her hand. "There I go again, more business jargon. I have to go check my messages, but I'll be back in a few minutes to see—"

But Amelia Bedelia was no longer listening. A curious look had come over her face. It was the look she got whenever she had a great idea, an urgent idea, an idea so bright that it flashed through her brain super fast and she could not wait one

more second to put it down on paper.

Amelia Bedelia was drawing so furiously that she barely noticed Sandy leaving the room or Mrs. Shauk circling the table.

She drew four large boxes, one in each corner of the paper. Inside each box she wrote two letters: BP, OP, PP, and CP. Then, in the center of the page, she drew a circle so big that it nearly touched the corners of every box. In the center of the circle she wrote two more letters: IP. Around the lower rim of that circle, she printed THINKING OUTSIDE THE BOX.

Amelia Bedelia drew as fast as she could, cramming as much detail as she could fit inside the circle. There were café

tables and chairs, a coffee bar, and an old-fashioned ice cream soda shop (the way she imagined it). There were gardens to grow healthy vegetables. There was a play structure made of huge industrial parts. There was a stage where people could perform, spaces to display things, and smaller areas with couches so people could sit and talk.

Amelia Bedelia leaned back in her chair to admire her handiwork. Then she made the mistake of looking to see what her classmates were doing. She spotted a lot of lists, with numbered ideas. She had only had *one* idea. She felt a little foolish.

Amelia Bedelia shook her head and folded her drawing first in

OP

IP

CP

outside the BOX

115

half, then in quarters. Then she scrunched it up with both hands into a ball. Glancing over her shoulder, she tossed her idea over her head toward the wastepaper basket by the door. Her wadded-up idea missed the basket, bounced off the wall, and rolled across the floor.

"Hey," said Clay. "Amelia Bedelia just tossed out an idea!"

Cliff jumped up and began dribbling her idea between his feet as if it was a soccer ball. "Look, he said. "I'm kicking an idea around!"

"Goofball," said Clay, reaching down to grab the scrunched-up paper. He

pretended to dribble away from the trash can and then whipped around and executed a jump shot that sent the paper ball arcing up, up, up—and straight into Mrs. Shauk's outstretched hand.

Chapter 13

What's the Big Idea?

Clay froze. No one else moved, either. Mrs. Shauk was clutching the bright white wad of paper with gleaming red fingernails, just like a hawk that had snatched a tiny bird out of the sky.

"No fair!" said Clay. "You were goaltending!"

"I was not," said Mrs. Shauk. "The

ball was still going up, not coming down."

"But—"

"I played on the basketball team in college, young man," said Mrs. Shauk.

Gosh, thought Amelia Bedelia. Our teacher is a basketball-playing French major with the eyesight of a hawk. No wonder we never get away with anything. . . .

"Now it's my turn," said

Mrs. Shauk, making the official referee hand sign. "I'm calling you for illegal procedure. You were goofing off when you should have been working."

"I was throwing out an idea," said Clay.

Just then, the conference-room door opened and Amelia Bedelia's father entered, along with a tall man in a dark blue suit, bright white shirt, and colorful bow tie. They stood together against the back wall, chatting quietly.

Mrs. Shauk tossed the wadded-up paper back to Clay and said, "Okay, let's hear your idea."

"But it isn't mine," said Clay, tossing the idea to Cliff.

"Cliff, go ahead," said Mrs. Shauk.

"It's not mine either," said Cliff.

"Whose idea is this?" asked Sandy.

No one even squeaked. They were not rats. They would never squeal on one another.

But Sandy and Mrs. Shauk were patient. The room was silent. Even Amelia Bedelia's father and the other man stopped talking.

Finally Amelia Bedelia slowly raised her arm. "That is . . . was . . . my idea,"

she said. "I tried to throw it out, for real, but missed. Clay was actually helping me throw it in the trash can."

"Looks like he threw it under a bus," said Amelia Bedelia's father.

Sandy smiled and said, "Well, if it doesn't embarrass you, Amelia Bedelia, would you share your idea with us?"

Amelia Bedelia nodded.

Cliff tossed the idea to Sandy, who uncurled the paper ball and held up the page.

"It's upside down," said Amelia Bedelia.

Amelia Bedelia's father took the paper, turned it around, and flattened it out as much as he could. He stuck pushpins in to hold it up on a corkboard, where everyone could see it. "Okay, sweetheart, we're all ears."

For a second, Amelia Bedelia imagined that every person in the room had turned

into a giant ear, ready to hear her say something dumb. She closed her eyes, took a deep breath, and with the same courage it takes to dive into an ice-cold lake, jumped up from her chair and began talking.

"Well, when you asked us for ideas outside the box, I didn't know what you meant. Do ideas come in a box?"

"I wish," said Amelia Bedelia's father. "I would order a case!"

Everyone laughed, helping Amelia Bedelia to relax a bit.

"It's hard to think about being outside the box," she said, "when we spend so much time in boxes. This room is a box. So is our classroom. This building is one big box."

The man with the bow tie standing

next to her father said, *"Hmmpf!"* He squinted his eyes at Amelia Bedelia and nodded his head.

Amelia Bedelia hoped he was agreeing with her, but she wasn't sure. She kept on talking anyway. "All the buildings around here are boxes. Offices, warehouses, factories—"

"Or plants," said Clay.

"Or plants," added Amelia Bedelia. "The signs say these are parks—business park, office park, professional park, and corporate park." As she named each one, she pointed to the squares on her drawing labeled BP, OP, PP, and CP. "But these parks aren't for playing at all. They're for working."

Dawn raised her hand. "What's that big circle in the middle? What do those letters I and P mean?" she asked.

"IP stands for idea park," said Amelia Bedelia.

I P = Idea Park

"Where's that?" asked Dawn.

"It doesn't exist . . . yet," said Amelia Bedelia. "That's my idea. To build a round building, not a box, with a glass dome for a roof. At night it would look like the top of a giant lightbulb."

"Like in cartoons," said Pat. "When a person in a cartoon gets an idea, a little lightbulb turns on over his head."

"Right," said Amelia Bedelia.

126

"This a park where you could get ideas. People who work in the boxes around here could come and share their ideas and get new ones. They could learn about the latest improvements. College professors and scientists and interesting people could come to talk about computers and technology and art and music . . . and there could be really good food. Maybe even a bakery."

"Sold!" boomed the man with the bow tie. He leaned forward and slapped the table with the palm of his hand. *POP!* Everyone jumped, including Amelia Bedelia's father.

Chapter 14

Do What You Want to Do!

The man in the bow tie walked to the front of the room.

"Everyone, I would like you to meet our client, Mr. Biggley," said Amelia Bedelia's father. "His company makes salad dressings."

"Before we talk about that," said Mr. Biggley, "I just want to say how impressed

I am with this young lady's idea." He shook Amelia Bedelia's hand. "That is the best example of outside-the-box thinking that I can recall. I'm glad your friends and teachers stopped you from throwing the baby out with the bathwater."

Amelia Bedelia looked around the room, including under the table. First a cat, now a baby and a bath. All invisible.

This was an interesting conference room.

"I'm meeting with the mayor next week," said Mr. Biggley. "He wants to talk about how the city can encourage businesses to move here. How about you come along and show him your idea?"

Amelia Bedelia's father was nodding

his head back and forth like a bobblehead.

"I think we can spare Amelia Bedelia from school to talk with the mayor," said Mrs. Shauk. "As long as she gives the class a full report when she gets back."

Amelia Bedelia sighed. She had known that an assignment would come her way sooner or later.

"Great!" said Mr. Biggley. "In the meantime, Amelia Bedelia, you may want to work out a few of the wrinkles in your plan."

"And creases," said Amelia Bedelia.

"I can help her with that," said Amelia Bedelia's father, smiling proudly.

"I also want to thank the entire class," said Mr. Biggley. "Your comments today gave us loads of insight into what young people would like in their salad dressings. We are planning to introduce a whole line of salad dressings just for kids. We figure that if kids actually like the taste of the dressing, they would eat more salads."

"That would be a healthy habit," said Mrs. Shauk. "Better than soda and candy."

"But will they taste as good as the dressings Amelia Bedelia's mom made?" said Dawn.

"We hope so," said Mr. Biggley. "We're hiring her to create the flavors and recipes."

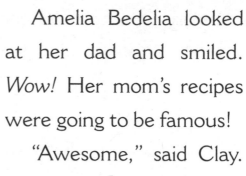

Amelia Bedelia looked at her dad and smiled. *Wow!* Her mom's recipes were going to be famous!

"Awesome," said Clay. "They taste like a skrillion."

"I like that line," said Mr. Biggley. "Tastes like a skrillion!"

"That might be a super tagline for an ad," said Amelia Bedelia's father, writing it down. "If we use your idea, Clay, you'll get credit. And payment."

"Yes!" said Clay, pumping his fists in the air.

Amelia Bedelia smiled as she thought about Clay getting paid to tag something. She

134

hoped her mom would make some actual money, not lettuce. Her mother already grew plenty of that.

After that, everyone got the chance to get up and present their ideas one by one. Amelia Bedelia liked listening to her friends. There were so many good ideas and so many possibilities and things to talk about and think about.

Best of all, no one said, "You can't do

that because it's never been done before"
or "You can't do that because you're too
young" or ". . . because you're a girl" or
". . . because you're a boy." From the way
her classmates were talking and smiling,
she could tell that they all had the same
feeling she did. Amelia Bedelia felt like
she could do anything she really wanted
to do.

Two Ways to Say It ♥
By Amelia Bedelia

"The goose that lays the golden eggs."

"The thing that makes a lot of money."

"She's a bean counter."

"She keeps track of money and numbers."

"Get your foot in the door."

"Start with an easy job, then learn and work hard."

"It's time for a cat nap."

"It's time for a short, refreshing nap."

"We are in the black!"

"We have made a profit!"

"You are in your salad days."

"You are young and fresh."

"He threw it under the bus."

"He gave it up for something he cared more about."

"Toss out ideas and kick them around."

"Share ideas and improve them by talking about them."

"Don't throw the baby out with the bathwater!"

"Try to think outside the box."

"Try to come up with new and different ideas."

"Don't throw away good parts when you get rid of bad parts."

Meet Amelia Bedelia and her friends!

Brad
Charlie
Joy
Daisy
me!
Holly
Rose
Suzanne
Willow
Gracie
Penny
Angel
Dawn
Heather

Finally

I ♥ MY DOG

Pierre

#10

Amelia Bedelia

Ties the Knot

by Herman Parish   pictures by Lynne Avril

#10

Hi!
Turn the page
for a special
sneak peek
at my next
adventure!

Chapter 1

A ~~Spring~~ sparkle in Her ~~Step~~ Eye

When Amelia Bedelia got home from school, there was a familiar car in their driveway. She jumped off her bike and ran inside, shouting, "Aunt Mary? Jason? Where are you?"

"In the kitchen!" called her mother.

Amelia Bedelia was so happy she began skipping. She skipped through the living room to the kitchen. Her mother and aunt were talking in low voices. The only word she caught was "notices."

Amelia Bedelia skipped to her aunt and gave her a giant hug.

"Hi, sweetie," said Mary. "It's great to see you again."

Aunt Mary and her mother were having an afternoon treat. "Pour yourself some lemonade while I cut up fruit," said her mother.

Amelia Bedelia looked around. She stuck her head into the dining room. "Is Jason hiding in here?" she asked. "I hate it when he jumps out and scares me." She kind of liked the thrill too, but she would never tell anyone that.

"No, your cousin couldn't come," said Mary. "He loves to stay after school for sports. The only thing he's jumping for is joy. What's new in school for you, Amelia Bedelia?"

"We just started studying flight and airplanes," said Amelia Bedelia.

With
Amelia Bedelia
anything can happen!

Have you read
them all?

Amelia Bedelia wants a new bike—a brand-new shiny, beautiful, fast bike just like Suzanne's new bike. Amelia Bedelia's dad says that a bike like that is really expensive and will cost an arm and a leg. Amelia Bedelia doesn't want to give away one of her arms and one of her legs. She'll need both arms to steer her new bike, and both legs to pedal it.

Amelia Bedelia is going to get a puppy—a sweet, adorable, loyal, friendly puppy! When her parents ask her what kind of dog she'd like, Amelia Bedelia doesn't know what to say. There are hundreds and thousands of dogs in the world, maybe even millions!

#3

Amelia Bedelia is hitting the road. Where is she going? It's a surprise! But one thing is certain. Amelia Bedelia and her mom and dad will try new things (like fishing), they'll eat a lot of pizza (yum), and Amelia Bedelia will meet a new friend—a friend she'll never, *ever* forget.

#4

Amelia Bedelia has an amazing idea! She is going to design and build a zoo in her backyard. Better yet, she is going to invite all her friends to bring their pets and help plan the exhibits and rides.

#5

Amelia Bedelia usually loves recess. One day, though, she doesn't get picked for a team and she begins to have second thoughts about sports. What's so great about racing and jumping and catching, anyway?

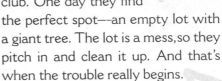

Amelia Bedelia and her friends are determined to find a cool clubhouse, maybe even a tree house, for their new club. One day they find the perfect spot—an empty lot with a giant tree. The lot is a mess, so they pitch in and clean it up. And that's when the trouble really begins.

Amelia Bedelia is so excited to be spending her vacation at the beach! She loves hanging out with her cousin Jason—especially since he's really great at surfing and knows so many kids in town. But one night, Amelia Bedelia sees Jason sneaking out the window. Where is he going? What is he up to?

Amelia Bedelia does not want to take dance classes. She loves to dance for fun, but ballet is not her cup of tea, and she is sure that Dana's School of Dance will be super boring. But guess what? Surprising teachers, new steps, cool kids, and even a pesky ballet bun inspire Amelia Bedelia and her classmates to dance up a storm!

Amelia Bedelia and her classmates are learning about occupations and jobs at school, and that means they go on some really interesting field trips. What does Amelia Bedelia want to be when she grows up? Turns out, the sky's the limit!

Hooray!

It's a dog's life

It's raining cats and dogs

The dog ate my homework